CHRISTMAS
TIME

Alison Jay

templar publishing

Christmas Eve

mistletoe

mittens

candle

card

stocking

reindeer

Father Christmas

sleigh

carol singers

snowman

polar bear

The North Pole

Christmas pudding

elves

workshop

snow globe

toys

presents

sack

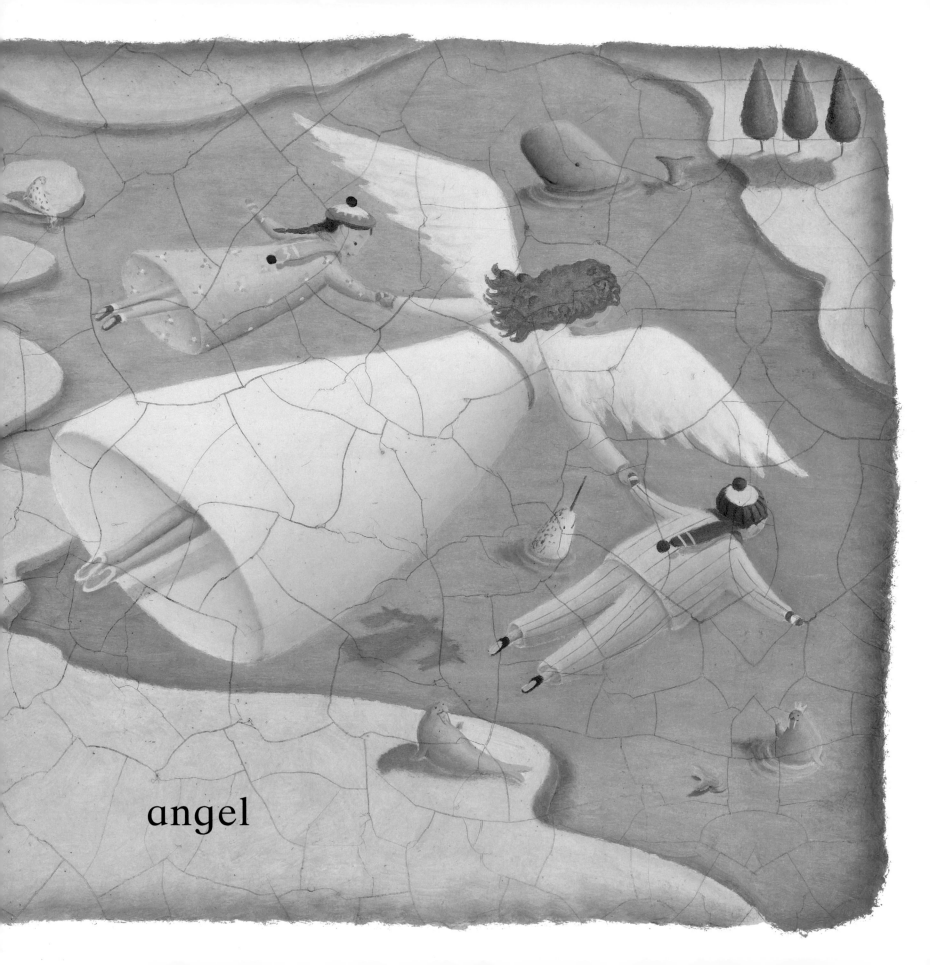

angel

baubles

Christmas tree

Christmas Day

1

2

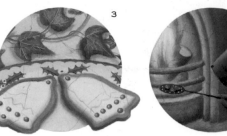
3

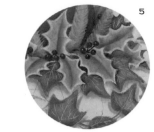
4

5

6

7

20

19

8

18

9

DID YOU SPOT THE HIDDEN LINKS TO CHRISTMAS SONGS IN THE PICTURES?

'TWAS THE NIGHT BEFORE CHRISTMAS
...and all through the house, not a creature
was stirring, not even a mouse. (1)

RUDOLPH THE RED-NOSED REINDEER (2)

SILVER BELLS (3)

THE CHRISTMAS SONG
Chestnuts roasting on an open fire... (4)

THE HOLLY AND THE IVY (5)

THE TWELVE DAYS OF CHRISTMAS
...five golden rings (6) ...two turtle doves (7)
and a partridge in a pear tree. (8)

WHILE SHEPHERDS
WATCHED THEIR FLOCKS (9)

GOOD KING WENCESLAS (10)

FROSTY THE SNOWMAN (11)

I SAW THREE SHIPS COME SAILING IN (12)

JINGLE BELLS
...oh what fun it is to ride in a one-horse open sleigh. (13)

SANTA CLAUS IS COMING TO TOWN (14)

LITTLE DRUMMER BOY (15)

LITTLE DONKEY (16)

WE THREE KINGS OF ORIENT ARE (17)
O star of wonder, star of night... (18)

HARK THE HERALD ANGELS SING (19)

AWAY IN A MANGER (20)

FOR DAVID, DOLLY, MILLY AND MR SPARKLER (AKA MR AND MRS CHRISTMAS)
AND HELPERS. LOVE FROM ALISON (BIRDY)

A TEMPLAR BOOK
First published in the UK in 2010 by Templar Publishing,
www.templarco.co.uk

Illustration copyright © 2010 by Alison Jay • Text and design copyright © 2010 by The Templar Company Limited

First edition • All rights reserved

ISBN: 978-1-84877-063-8

Designed by janie louise hunt • Concept by Libby Hamilton • Edited by Libby Hamilton

Printed in China

10

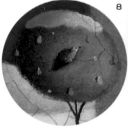
11

17

16

15

14

13

12